CHADRON (NE) STATE COLLEGE

3 5086 00346481 3

MAR 15 1993

W9-BJV-322

Serena Katz

For Jennifer Dent and Lillian Solis —C.P.

For Fritz —R.W.A.

Serena Katz

BY CHARLOTTE POMERANTZ

ILLUSTRATED BY R. W. ALLEY

MACMILLAN PUBLISHING COMPANY   NEW YORK

MAXWELL MACMILLAN CANADA   TORONTO

MAXWELL MACMILLAN INTERNATIONAL

NEW YORK   OXFORD   SINGAPORE   SYDNEY

RETA E. KING LIBRARY
CHADRON STATE COLLEGE
CHADRON, NE 69337

Nestled snugly in the Pocono Mountains was the town of Elmsville. It was a little town of neat wooden houses, mostly painted white, with a few painted gray or brown.

One house was different. It was yellow all over, with blue shutters, black trim, and an orange roof. It was the home of the Duncan family: Mrs. Duncan, Mr. Duncan, and their children, Peter and Molly.

Mr. Duncan was a paint salesman. He sold paint by traveling all over the country and being friendly to his customers.

But that is not how he met Serena Katz. He met her over the phone. She worked in a hardware store in New York City and she was one of his best customers.

Whenever he phoned her to see if she needed any paint, she asked him what was new in colors.

Luscious Lemon is big this year, he would say. Or, Lobster Red. Or, Banana Surprise.

Yummy, Serena Katz would say. And she would order twenty gallons of each.

One time, after she had placed a special order for Raspberry Riot, she inquired whether Mr. Duncan and his family had ever visited New York City.

No, said Mr. Duncan. He and Mrs. Duncan had often talked about it. Molly was nine now and Peter was eight. Maybe some weekend…

"Well," said Serena Katz, "whenever you decide to come, send me a postcard. And I'll send a postcard back. I live on the ground floor of a brownstone. There's lots of room and I love company."

And that's how the Duncans decided to spend a weekend in New York City.

"By gum," said Mrs. Kartoffle, the postmistress, when the Duncans came to pick up their mail, "you folks got a postcard from Serena Katz."

She put on her glasses to read it. "She's expecting you this weekend."

"Do you always read our mail?" asked Peter.

Mrs. Kartoffle looked offended. "Only the postcards," she said.

Handing over the card she remarked, "Serena Katz was the best pool player on the West Side."

"I don't think it's the same Serena Katz," said Mr. Duncan. "This one works in a hardware store. She sells paint."

Mrs. Kartoffle arched her back as if she were holding a cue stick behind her. Then, leaning backwards over an imaginary pool table, she said, "Serena Katz could hit the ball, bounce it off a cushion, and *pow*! it would sail right into the pocket."

She straightened up and shook her head. "What a woman. People called her the Katz Meow."

When Molly told her friend Jenny that she was going to New York City and staying with a woman named Serena Katz, Jenny stared at her open-mouthed.

"Serena Katz!" she exclaimed. "I'd give anything to know how she pulls those gerbils out of her ears."

"Gerbils?" said Molly.

"You know," said Jenny. "Those beady-eyed little creatures that look like mice. Only they're not mice. They're gerbils."

"I wonder if it's the same Serena Katz," mumbled Molly.

E. KING LIBRARY
CHADRON STATE COLLEGE
CHADRON, NE 69337

After dinner, Mrs. Duncan and the children sat down at a game of dominoes with Mr. Korten, the school librarian.

"Before we start to play," said Mr. Korten, "are there any questions?"

"Yes," said Peter. "Do you know Serena Katz?"

The box of dominoes fell with a clatter. "Serena Katz? Not *the* Serena Katz!"

Peter shrugged. "Maybe not."

"Nonsense," said Mr. Korten. "There's only one Serena Katz. The hottest pistol I ever saw on a motorcycle. Krazy Katz, we called her. Krazy with a *K*, that is."

Mrs. Duncan fidgeted in her seat. "Did—uh—Krazy Katz ever work in a hardware store?"

Mr. Korten had risen from his seat and was gesturing excitedly. "There wasn't anything she couldn't ride. Harley-Davidson. Honda. Suzuki. You name it, she raced it. Once she spurted up a ramp, rose thirty feet in the air, and jumped over three parked buses. Fantastic!"

His voice softened. "She always tucked a yellow rose into her crash helmet. At the end of the race, she would toss it to some fellow in the crowd."

Mr. Korten paused and colored slightly. "I caught it once," he said.

"I hear you are going to visit Serena Katz," called out Mr. Talleyrand, the garbage collector, when he came by in his truck.

"That's right," said Mrs. Duncan. "Do you know her, too?"

"Who doesn't," said Mr. Talleyrand. "Her wedding cakes are famous all over New York City."

Mrs. Duncan started to say, "Maybe it's not the same—" Instead, she said, "I didn't know she made wedding cakes."

Mr. Talleyrand turned off the motor of his truck.

"Serena Katz didn't *make* wedding cakes," he said. "She *created* them, spun them out of her fancy. There would be three layers. And on the top, just above those little bride and groom dolls, there was a tiny fountain, with real water lit up by colored lights."

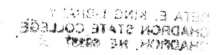
RETA E. KING LIBRARY
CHADRON STATE COLLEGE
CHADRON, NE 69337

RETA E. KING LIBRARY
CHADRON STATE COLLEGE
CHADRON, NE 69337

When the Duncan family rang the doorbell of the brownstone in New York City, a little old lady, spry as a grasshopper, met them at the door.

"Hello," she chirped. "You must be the Duncans. Come on in and I'll show you around."

The Duncans nodded dumbly and followed her down the hall.

"Molly and Peter will sleep in this room. It's Tuna Fish Pink. Mr. and Mrs. Duncan, this is your room. It's Fuzzy Peach. And my room is—" she flung open the door.

"Don't tell me," said Mr. Duncan. "Raspberry Riot."

Serena Katz smiled. "It's nice to meet a paint salesman who knows his colors."

As soon as the Duncans had unpacked, she handed them a picnic lunch and a list of places to visit. "Now don't waste your time with an old lady like me," she said. "There's a big beautiful city out there. Have fun."

The Duncans visited the Brooklyn Museum, the South Street Seaport, the penny arcade in Times Square, and the Museum of the American Indian. Over their picnic lunch, they decided to ask Serena Katz about the other Serena Katzes. But when they got back to the brownstone, they were so tired that they flopped into their beds and fell asleep.

The next morning at breakfast they tried to ask a few questions, but Serena Katz brushed them aside. "You didn't come all the way to New York City to hear the story of my life." Handing them their coats and a list of more places to visit, she opened the front door and said, "Out you go."

The Duncans marveled at the beauty of the Brooklyn Botanic Garden, the view from the silent, soaring tramway which crosses the East River to Roosevelt Island, and the quiet loveliness of the Tibetan Temple on Staten Island.

They also took the ferry to see the Statue of Liberty, but they hadn't even reached Miss Liberty's kneecap when they turned back and walked down. Exhausted, they went back to the city and stumbled into a movie theater. Mr. and Mrs. Duncan sat through two showings of *Ghostbusters* while Molly and Peter slept.

Brooklyn Public Library

"I don't suppose it's any of my business," said Mrs. Duncan, "but did you ever ride a motorcycle?"

"Didn't *ride* them," said Serena Katz. "*Raced* them." She giggled. "You'll never guess what they used to call me."

"Krazy Katz," said Mrs. Duncan. "Krazy with a *K*, that is."

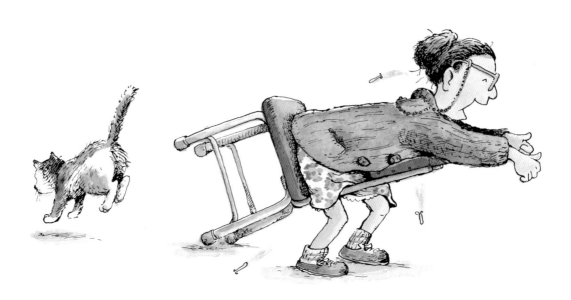

Serena Katz beamed modestly. "You wouldn't believe how proud I was of the name. But the races made my gerbils so nervous that I had to quit. That's when I took up wedding cakes and lion taming. On my days off, of course."

"Of course," said the Duncans, who couldn't take their eyes off her.

She looked at her watch. "Time for bed," she said. "I have to go to work tomorrow."

As they all helped her clean up the kitchen, Mr. Duncan said, "You *do* work in the hardware store, don't you?"

"Every day, except Saturdays and Sundays. From nine to five."

Early the next morning, the Duncans stood with their luggage in the hallway of the brownstone.

"My dear Serena Katz," said Mrs. Duncan, "we've had the best time ever."

"Now you must come visit us in Elmsville," said Molly.

"It's in the heart of the Poconos," said Mr. Duncan. "About two hours by train."

"By train," said Serena Katz. "That's an idea."

"Or you can take the bus directly to Elmsville," said Mrs. Duncan.

Serena Katz scratched her ear thoughtfully. "A bus," she said. "Now that's another idea."

Peter looked at her anxiously. "You will come, won't you?" he said.

"Promise!" said Molly.

Serena Katz smiled. An impish faraway smile. "I will," she said. "And I never break a promise."

One Sunday afternoon when the Duncan's were outside their house, a hot-air balloon landed in their backyard.

"Hi," said Serena Katz, leaning over the basket. "I told you I'd come."

"How did you know it was our house?" said Molly.

"I could just tell," said Serena Katz.